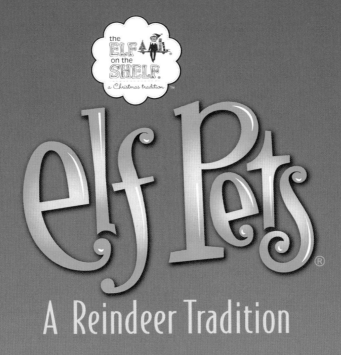

A Reindeer Tradition

Creatively Classic Activities and Books®

For Christa

—CAB

Published by
CCA & B, LLC.
3350 Riverwood Parkway SE, Suite 300
Atlanta, GA 30339

http://www.elfontheshelf.com

First Edition
10 9 8 7 6 5 4 3 2

Library of Congress Cataloging-in-Publication Data

Bell, Chanda A.
    Elf Pets®: A Reindeer Tradition / written by Chanda A. Bell-- 1st ed.
        p. cm.
Summary: When Santa's sleigh at the North Pole won't fly, Santa enlists the help of The Elf on the Shelf® scout elves and their Elf Pets®—reindeer who carry a heart charm filled with Christmas magic activated by the hope of children who truly believe. Storybook, reindeer and magical heart charm included.
–Provided by Publisher

ISBN-13: 978-0-9843651-8-0
ISBN-10: 0-9843651-8-4

the ELF on the SHELF®
a Christmas tradition™

elf Pets®

A Reindeer Tradition

by
Chanda A. Bell

W here the moon gently cast a bright bluish glow
And the forest was wrapped in a new-fallen snow,
The animals gathered to see for themselves
The take-off and landing of Santa's scout elves.

Each Elf on the Shelf in its red and white suit

Leaped and spun 'round with each trumpeters toot;

And drumbeats resounded with **"rat-a-tat-tat"**

While elves in the air flew this way and that.

All creatures and critters no matter their size,

Marvelled at what they'd just seen with their eyes.

They all seemed to know how special it is

To work for Kris Kringle and hang out with kids.

The animals turned to the stable nearby.
A **"c-r-a-s-h!"** could be heard and a faint little cry.

Out the door they all tumbled like dice in a game;

'Twas the nine mighty reindeer, each known by his name.

Above all their heads the sleigh flew through the air,

Then landed **"ker-plunk"** right next to a bear.

Santa turned to his side, shook his head with regret,
"Let's try this again. We can't give up yet!"
The elves stood in silence. The animals did, too.
The sleigh was not flying. What could they do?

The reindeer tried harder…the elves' eyes grew round…
But the sleigh did not budge, not an inch off the ground.
"Christmas Spirit is needed to make the sleigh soar,"
Santa said with a sadness they'd not heard before.

In the blink of an eye, the sleigh lifted mid-air.

"Someone believes," Santa noted with care.

It lasted a moment then back to the ground.
"Thump!" the sleigh hit. The elves glanced around.
Santa looked to the stable, and right through the door
Stood thousands of reindeer pawing the floor.

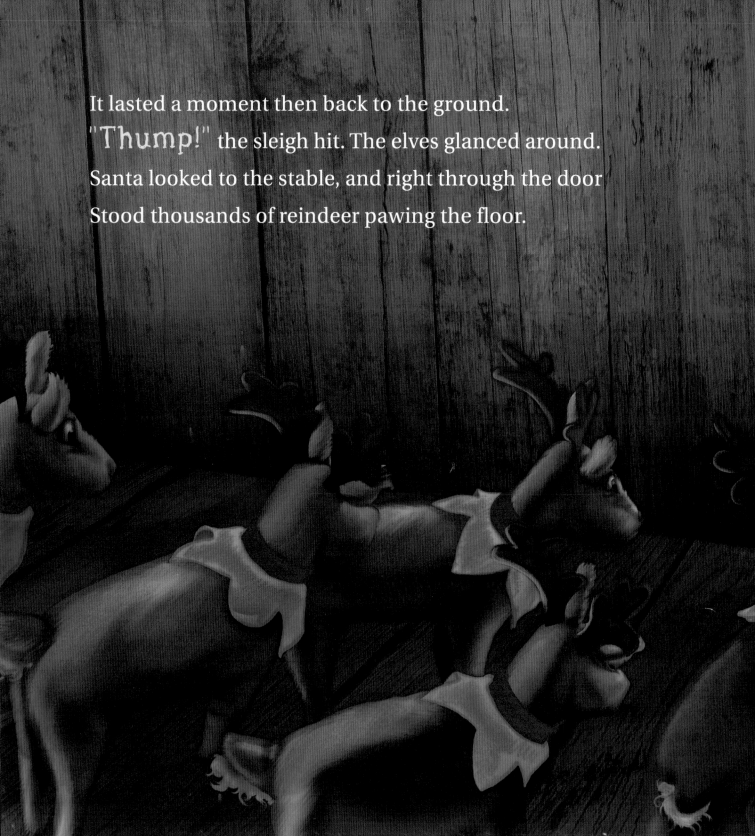

At once they stepped forward, as if to say,
"Santa, choose us to help pull the sleigh!"
Santa chuckled and said, "My friendly elf pets,
This task would be big—as big as it gets!"

The scout elves then shouted, "Don't count them out!

They're tiny like us, but we have no doubt

The kids would adopt them, and give them a name.

They'll treat them like us—one and the same."

Santa listened to stories the scout elves recounted—
All the moments of faith, hope and love they'd encountered.
While out on assignment, the big and the small
Proved the spirit of Christmas was alive, after all!

"Perhaps with more reindeer and faith that is true
We'd build Christmas magic to help the sleigh through
The dangers that often stand in the way
Of delivering presents by Christmas day."

Santa turned to the reindeer and stretched out his arm.

In his palm he revealed a tiny heart charm.

"The hope of all children who believe in their heart

In the magic of Christmas will make my sleigh start.

Wear this charm proudly for people to see.

It should serve to remind them your mission's for me.

Let them hold you and love you as much as they can.

This heart holds your magic. Do you understand?

You see, it's not fragile—not like an elf.

Your goal's not the same—to watch from a shelf.

Your job is to snuggle and nestle up tight,

To store up the wonder that makes me take flight.

The night before Christmas once sleep has come,
The sleigh will approach and you will become
A fully grown reindeer—brilliant and grand
While magic swirls softly like wind-blown sand.

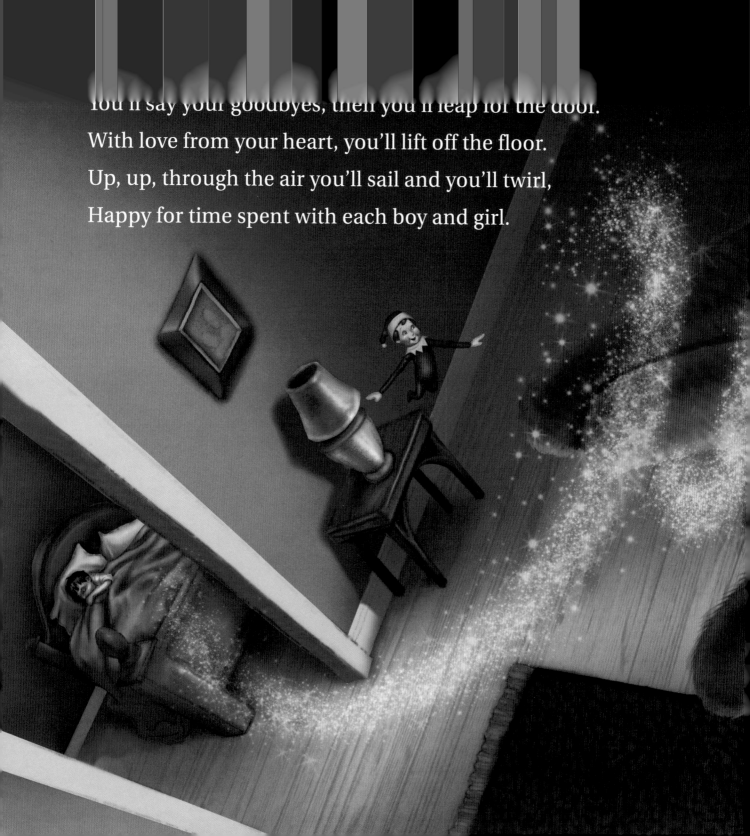

You'll say your goodbyes, then you'll leap for the door.
With love from your heart, you'll lift off the floor.
Up, up, through the air you'll sail and you'll twirl,
Happy for time spent with each boy and girl.

We'll meet on the roof and you'll take your place
As part of the team that makes my sleigh race.
Over the rooftops and high above mountains
Crossing the rivers, we'll dance over fountains.

My sleigh will bring joy on Christmas Eve
Thanks to each reindeer and kids who believe!"

We welcomed our Elf Pets® Reindeer on

_December 4_____ , 20 _15_ .

We chose the name:

_Mistletoe_____

We promise to love and hug
our Elf Pets® Reindeer
to help Santa's sleigh fly.